A CHRISTMAS CATASTROPHE!

Written and Illustrated by

Michelle Lawrence

AuthorHouse™
1663 Liberty Drive
Bloomington, IN 47403
www.authorhouse.com
Phone: 1 (800) 839-8640

Published by AuthorHouse 03/23/2019

ISBN: 978-1-7283-0445-8 (sc)
ISBN: 978-1-7283-0509-7 (hc)
ISBN: 978-1-7283-0446-5 (e)

Print information available on the last page.

This book is printed on acid-free paper.

authorHOUSE®

About the Author

Michelle Lawrence has been writing stories since she could spell.

She is ten years old today, yet she writes stories.
She also illustrated this book. Her father taught her how to draw.
She was raised in Chester, Pennsylvania and she lived there since birth.
At age ten, she moved to Austell, Georgia.

About the Book

Michelle was a very creative, artistic child. She would retreat to her room for hours to create.

I would find all kinds of treasures in her trash can, and she would just shrug her shoulders! I realized early on that this was no ordinary talent and that Michelle had something extraordinary!

The Christmas Catastrophe! was one of those finds. That year, Michelle was only ten years old, and she was so embarrassed when I sent copies of her work to the family in lieu of Christmas cards.

A Christmas Catastrophe was recently resurrected while going through old cabinets and closets, and upon reading it, it again held my attention until the very end and brought a great smile to my face and warmth to my heart.

I decided that the world could use a smile and some warmth, and as a gift to Michelle, to have it published for years to come and maybe even someday be read when she has children of her own!

I love you, pretty girl!

—Mom

Contents

Chapter 1

"Mom!" Shouted Crystal, one December morning.
"I can't find my stocking. Here's yours, Dad's, Chris's, and Cindy's!"
She went through the box tossing ornaments here and there.
"It's not in this big box!"

"Well, look in the small box!" Mrs. Robinson shouted back.
"Oh, here it is." Crystal said to herself.

She marched up the cellar stairs, feeling foolish because she did not see something that was right under her nose.

CHRIS

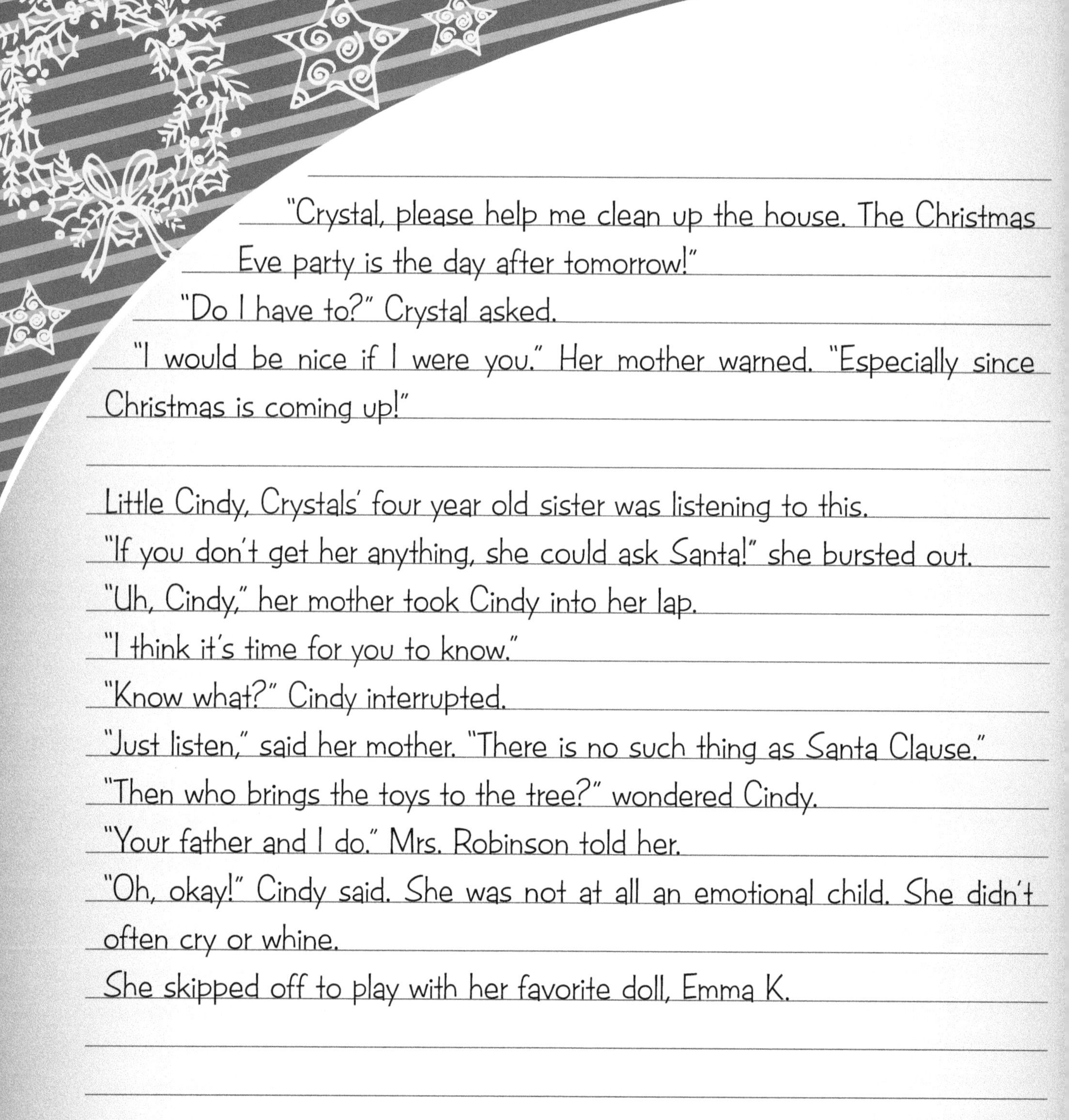

"Crystal, please help me clean up the house. The Christmas Eve party is the day after tomorrow!"

"Do I have to?" Crystal asked.

"I would be nice if I were you." Her mother warned. "Especially since Christmas is coming up!"

Little Cindy, Crystals' four year old sister was listening to this.
"If you don't get her anything, she could ask Santa!" she bursted out.
"Uh, Cindy," her mother took Cindy into her lap.
"I think it's time for you to know."
"Know what?" Cindy interrupted.
"Just listen," said her mother. "There is no such thing as Santa Clause."
"Then who brings the toys to the tree?" wondered Cindy.
"Your father and I do." Mrs. Robinson told her.
"Oh, okay!" Cindy said. She was not at all an emotional child. She didn't often cry or whine.
She skipped off to play with her favorite doll, Emma K.

Just then, Chris, Crystal's older brother came down the stairs.

"Sup," he said.

The doorbell rang. It was Sylvia, Chris's date to the party he was going to. Crystal watched from the kitchen.

She was beautiful, and she had big, brown eyes, great hair, and a perfect body.

Crystal compared herself to Sylvia.

She now felt ugly and plain.

Crystal had strait black hair, while Sylvia's was krimpy and brown.

She knew now why Chris was dating her.

Chris and Sylvia left the house, looking great together.

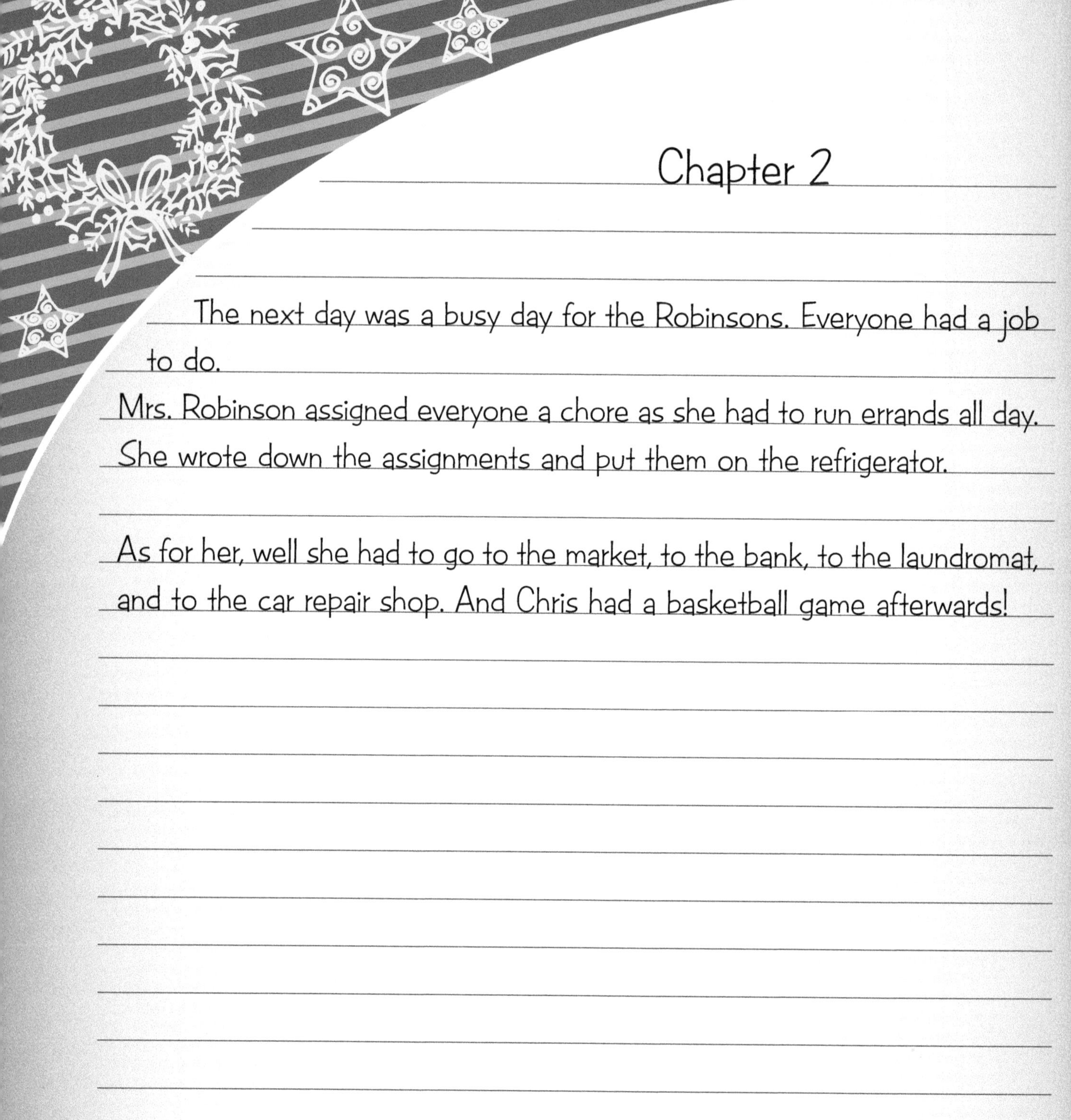

Chapter 2

The next day was a busy day for the Robinsons. Everyone had a job to do.

Mrs. Robinson assigned everyone a chore as she had to run errands all day. She wrote down the assignments and put them on the refrigerator.

As for her, well she had to go to the market, to the bank, to the laundromat, and to the car repair shop. And Chris had a basketball game afterwards!

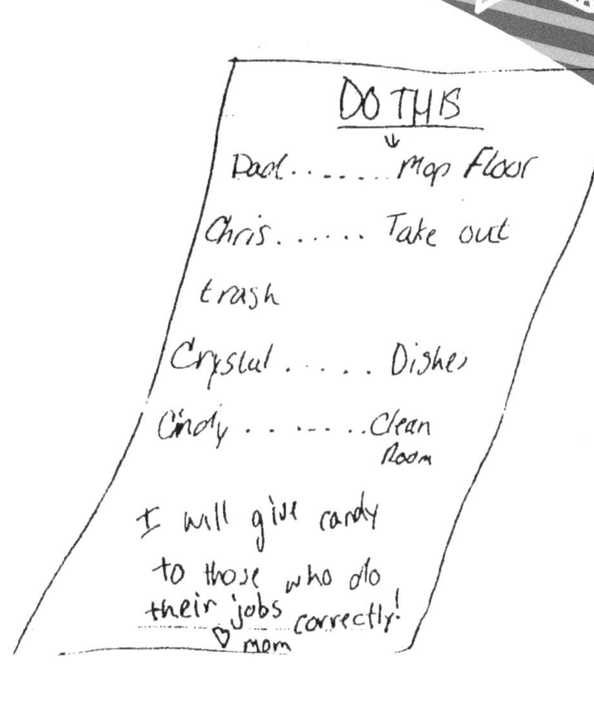
DO THIS
Dad...... Mop Floor
Chris..... Take out trash
Crystal..... Dishes
Cindy....... Clean Room
I will give candy to those who do their jobs correctly!
♡ mom

Chris's game was a success! He was playing against the Whips. The ending score was Eagles forty-two and Whips thirty-four.

Chris, as usual, kept on his hat and sunglasses. His coaches had no problems with it. He still played great. His position is point guard.

Afterward, the Robinsons went to McDonalds for lunch. Mr. Robinson had a meeting to go to at six-thirty p.m. For supper, they had lasagna.

Chapter 3

Today is the day of the Christmas Eve Party. Everyone will come.

The Robinsons were decorating when Mrs. Robinson's rich, elderly sister came in with her children.

"Well, well, young short-of-money people," teased the aunt. "What's this? Plastic ware instead of crystal ware?"

"Well, it's not a feast! I'm no dippy! What's the use of spending a bunch of money on some junk that we'll never use? I'm fed up with you! My husbands fed up with you! If you're going to complain, take your bratty children and get out of my house!" Shouted Mrs. Robinson.

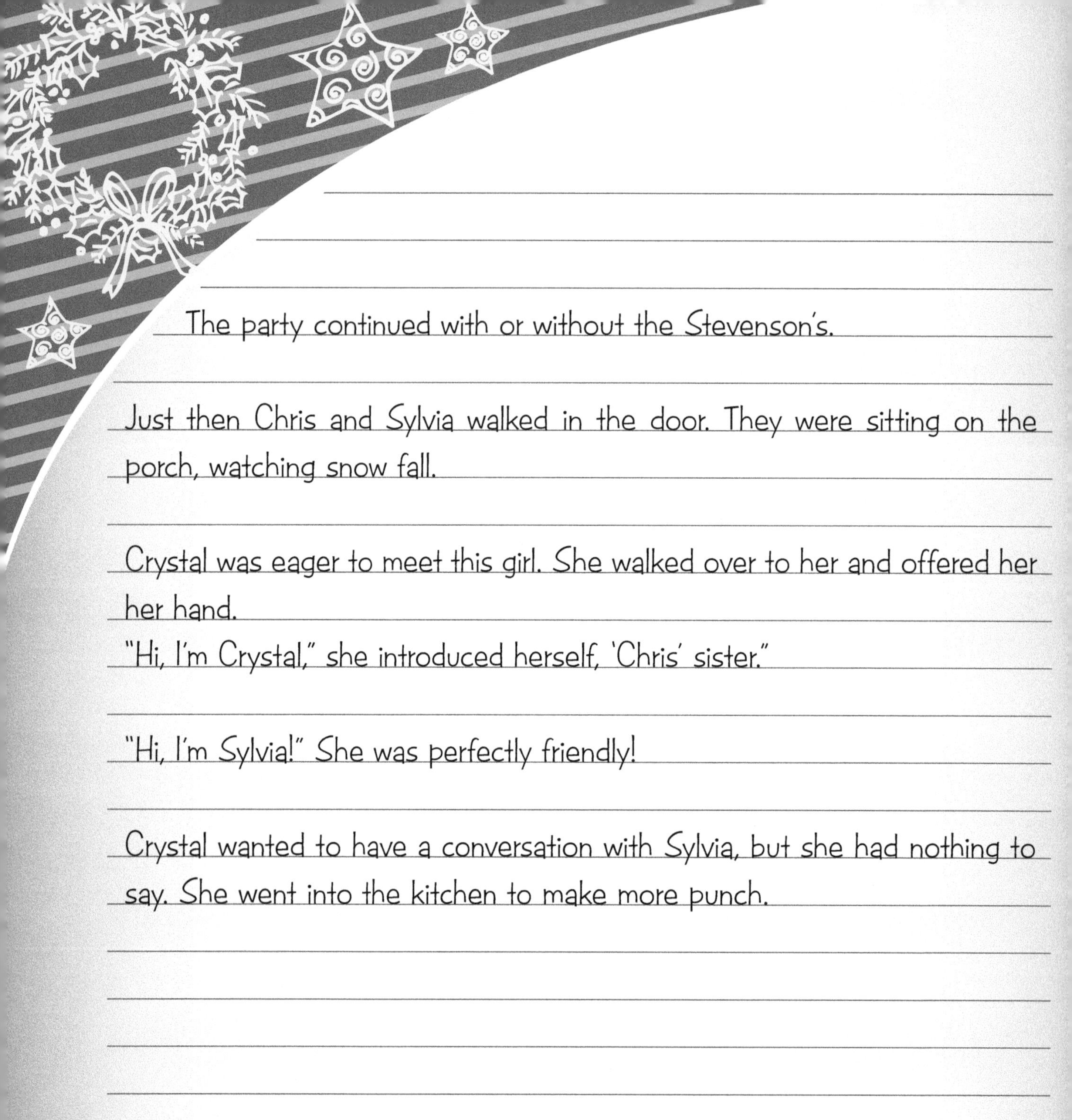

The party continued with or without the Stevenson's.

Just then Chris and Sylvia walked in the door. They were sitting on the porch, watching snow fall.

Crystal was eager to meet this girl. She walked over to her and offered her her hand.
"Hi, I'm Crystal," she introduced herself, 'Chris' sister."

"Hi, I'm Sylvia!" She was perfectly friendly!

Crystal wanted to have a conversation with Sylvia, but she had nothing to say. She went into the kitchen to make more punch.

The party soon ended and everyone went home.

The Christmas tree shone brightly in the corner. For a while it did. Then, all of a sudden the lights on the tree went out.

"Oh no" said Mr. Robinson. "Another Christmas Catastrophe."

"Well, children," said Mrs. Robinson, 'off to bed. The sooner you go to bed, the sooner Christmas will come."That night, Crystal dreamed of Christmas. She dreamt that no one would come over tomorrow, and that she would only get one present.

She woke up in the middle of the night and laid on her back staring at the ceiling.

She fell asleep again, and dreamt of Sylvia and her beauty.

Chapter 4

Crystal peeled her eyes open drearily. She had a feeling that she was supposed to be excited. Then, it hit her. It's Christmas!

"She jumped out of bed and ran downstairs. Her excitement slipped away. There stood a tree that was not lit, AND it had nothing under it. She was ready to cry.

She blinked back her tears and walked upstairs. 'We're not having Christmas," she thought, "Wait until I tell Chris and Cindy."

She walked towards her parents' room. "Mom, Dad, what about Christmas?" She wanted to know. 'Wha....." her father stumbled. "Oh, no! Another Christmas Catastrophe!"

"We forgot to put the presents under the tree!" Shouted her mother. "Go back to bed, and we'll wake you when it's time."

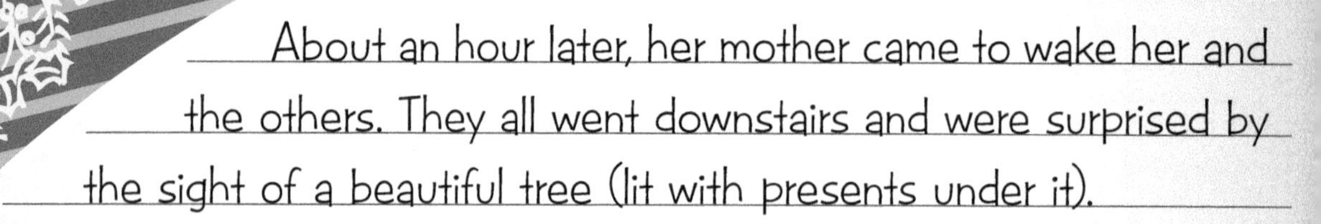

About an hour later, her mother came to wake her and the others. They all went downstairs and were surprised by the sight of a beautiful tree (lit with presents under it).

They all sat down opening presents. Wrapping paper was everywhere. Mr. Robinson got a gold watch and a new suit. Mrs. Robinson got a silver ring, necklace, and earrings. Chris got a basketball, a radio, a skateboard, and tennis shoes. Crystal got some new outfits, a doll house, and two dolls. And Cindy got a doll, tennis shoes, and a My Size Barbie doll. Everyone was satisfied.

Crystal had a question that was burning inside of her. She asked, "Dad, what's a Christmas Catastrophe?" Mr. Robinson answered, "You wouldn't understand if I told you!"
The Robinsons all laughed and had a Merry Christmas.

YOU HAVE ONE, TOO!

The End!

CPSIA information can be obtained
at www.ICGtesting.com
Printed in the USA
BVHW020956040419
544608BV00018B/155/P